TRANSCENDING RACE IN AMERICA
BIOGRAPHIES OF BIRACIAL ACHIEVERS

Halle Berry

Beyoncé

David Blaine

Mariah Carey

Frederick Douglass

W. E. B. Du Bois

Salma Hayek

Derek Jeter

Alicia Keys

Soledad O'Brien

Rosa Parks

Prince

Booker T. Washington

FREDERICK DOUGLASS

Abolitionist, Author, Editor, and Diplomat

Jim Whiting

Mason Crest Publishers

Produced by 21st Century Publishing and Communications, Inc.

MASON CREST PUBLISHERS INC.
370 Reed Road
Broomall, Pennsylvania 19008
(866) MCP-BOOK (toll free)
www.masoncrest.com

Printed in the United States of America.

First Printing

9 8 7 6 5 4 3 2 1

Library of Congress Cataloging-in-Publication Data

Whiting, Jim, 1943–
    Frederick Douglass / Jim Whiting.
      p. cm. —(Transcending race in America. Biographies of biracial achievers)
    Includes bibliographical references and index.
    ISBN 978-1-4222-1611-8 (hardback : alk. paper) — ISBN 978-1-4222-1625-5 (pbk. : alk. paper)
    1. Douglass, Frederick, 1818–1895—Juvenile literature. 2. Abolitionists—United States—
Biography—Juvenile literature. 3. African American abolitionists—Biography—Juvenile
literature. 4. Antislavery movements—United States—Juvenile literature. I. Title.
E449.D75W48 2010
973.8092—dc22
[B]   2009023991

Publisher's notes:
All quotations in this book come from original sources, and contain the spelling and grammatical inconsistencies
of the original text.

The Web sites mentioned in this book were active at the time of publication. The publisher is not responsible
for Web sites that have changed their addresses or discontinued operation since the date of publication. The
publisher will review and update the Web site addresses each time the book is reprinted.

Table of Contents

> " I HAVE BROTHERS, SISTERS, NIECES,
> NEPHEWS, UNCLES, AND COUSINS,
> OF EVERY RACE AND EVERY HUE,
> SCATTERED ACROSS THREE CONTINENTS,
> AND FOR AS LONG AS I LIVE,
> I WILL NEVER FORGET THAT
> IN NO OTHER COUNTRY ON EARTH
> IS MY STORY EVEN POSSIBLE. "

> " WE MAY HAVE DIFFERENT STORIES,
> BUT WE HOLD COMMON HOPES. . . .
> WE MAY NOT LOOK THE SAME
> AND WE MAY NOT HAVE
> COME FROM THE SAME PLACE,
> BUT WE ALL WANT TO MOVE
> IN THE SAME DIRECTION —
> TOWARDS A BETTER FUTURE . . . "

— BARACK OBAMA, 44TH PRESIDENT
OF THE UNITED STATES OF AMERICA

Chapter

1

❧ ❀ ❧

MAKING HIS VOICE HEARD

IN THE EARLY 1840S, ABOLITIONISTS, OR people living in the North who opposed slavery, flocked to meetings to hear speakers describe its evils. One of the star attractions was a young escaped slave named Frederick Douglass. He was a polished **orator** who held audiences spellbound with his graphic descriptions of the brutality he experienced.

Too polished, some people believed. Slaves were supposed to be ignorant and uneducated. Some listeners were especially **skeptical** because Frederick never gave any specific information about where he was from or how he had escaped.

To Frederick, there was only one way to make people believe he was telling the truth. He would write his autobiography. In it, he would name names and list details of his upbringing.

Frederick Douglass was still a young man when he began to speak out against the evils of slavery. Because he was an escaped slave, he put his life in danger when he made speeches because he could be recaptured and taken back to his master in the South.

RISKING HIS FREEDOM

Frederick was taking a huge risk. He had lived as a free man in the North for several years. But under the laws at that time, he still belonged to Thomas Auld, who had been his master in Maryland. Providing exact details could make it much easier for Auld to find him. If that happened, Frederick would be returned to the South and become a slave again.

Frederick was willing to take the risk. He had already discovered his purpose in life. When he first began attending abolitionist meetings, he was content to sit and listen to other people speak. Everything changed on August 11, 1841:

> **"I felt strongly moved to speak. . . . I spoke but a few moments, when I felt a degree of freedom, and said what I desired with considerable ease. From that time until now, I have been engaged in pleading the cause of my brethren."**

So in 1845, Frederick took the first step on a path he would never leave. He published *Narrative of the Life of Frederick Douglass, an American Slave.*

Another Famous Black Autobiography

At the end of the 19th century, Booker T. Washington was the most influential black man in the United States. He published his autobiography, *Up From Slavery*, in 1901.

The book begins with his childhood as a slave and his struggles to get an education when he was set free after the Civil War. At one point he walked almost 500 miles from his home to attend school. He later founded the Tuskegee Institute. It was one of the most important black schools in the late 19th and early 20th centuries.

Using his own experiences as a model, Washington emphasized hard work and self-reliance. White readers praised the book as a classic rags-to-riches story of traditional American values.

Many blacks thought Washington's book didn't come down hard enough on white racism. They also thought it encouraged blacks to try to fit into white society, rather than working toward attaining voting rights and social equality.

Booker T. Washington, another famous black writer who was born a slave, works in his office at Tuskegee Institute. His books said that blacks should work hard to fit into white America. Many people though he should have emphasized working toward voting rights instead.

White slave owners had long insisted blacks were inferior. They said slaves had good working and living conditions. In fact, the slave owners said, we're actually doing them a favor. We're giving them an education and introducing them to the Christian faith.

WHAT SLAVERY WAS REALLY LIKE

Frederick's *Narrative* exploded those myths and exposed the harsh realities of slavery. On the book's first page, Frederick pointed out that slaves were denied even small things his readers took for granted:

> "A want of information concerning my own [birthday] was a source of unhappiness to me even during childhood. The white children could tell their ages. I could not tell why I ought to be deprived of the same privilege."

Not knowing when they were born was just the start of a hard, brutal life for most slaves. Frederick described in detail an all-too-common practice:

Few people in the North knew that many slaves were whipped by their masters, as shown in this drawing. In 1845, Frederick's first book shocked the public with its many stories about the horrible things slaves had to endure. The success and popularity of the book led Frederick to leave the country to avoid being captured.

> **I have often been awakened at the dawn of day by the most heart-rending shrieks of an own aunt of mine, whom [a slave owner] used to tie up to a joist, and whip upon her naked back until she was literally covered with blood. . . . He would whip her to make her scream, and whip her to make her hush; and not until overcome by fatigue, would he cease to swing the blood-clotted cowskin.**

The book is filled with similar stories about the unhappy lives of slaves. For example, when Frederick's master died, his property was divided among his heirs. Slaves were part of this property. As Frederick somewhat bitterly recalled,

> **We were all ranked together at the valuation. Men and women, old and young, married and single, were ranked with horses, sheep and swine.**

That was humiliating. Far worse was the way in which slave owners broke up families. "A single word from the white men was enough . . . to **sunder** forever the dearest friends, dearest kindred, and strongest ties known to human beings," Frederick wrote. He mailed a copy to Auld himself, challenging him to **refute** what he had written.

SUCCESS LEADS TO DANGER

The book became very successful, but its success put Frederick in even greater danger of losing his freedom.

His friends thought he should flee the country. Great Britain seemed the best place for him to go. The country had abolished slavery in its vast empire in 1833.

It wasn't an easy decision. He would have to leave his wife and four children behind. As would happen often during his life, Frederick decided that his mission was the most important thing.

2

GROWING UP IN SLAVERY

FREDERICK'S MOTHER WAS A SLAVE NAMED Harriet Bailey. She belonged to a man named Aaron Anthony in Talbot County, Maryland. In turn, Anthony managed the very large estate of Edward Lloyd, a prominent landowner.

Anthony and Lloyd kept their slaves as ignorant as possible. Their slaves didn't even know their birthdays. Frederick thought he had been born in February, but he didn't know if it was in 1817 or 1818.

Harriet gave her son the important-sounding name of Frederick Augustus Washington Bailey. That was about all she was able to give him. Mother and son were soon separated and Frederick lived with his grandmother. His mother worked in fields 12 miles away. A few times she made the long walk to see him for a few hours. Frederick barely knew her.

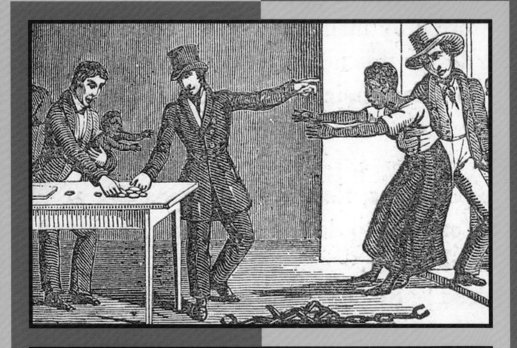

A 19th century drawing shows a slave baby being sold away from its mother. Frederick suffered the same fate, and as a child he rarely saw his mother. He lived with his grandmother, but she left him with his owner when he was seven years old.

A LIFELONG MYSTERY

Frederick knew even less about his father. In the *Narrative*, he wrote, "My father was a white man. He was admitted to be such by all I ever heard speak of my parentage." Frederick's skin was lighter than his mother or his grandmother's, so that was probably true.

He never learned who his father was. When he was in his 60s, he wrote,

> "Of my father I know nothing. Slavery had no recognition of fathers, as none of families. That the mother was a slave was enough for its deadly purpose. By its law the child followed the condition of its mother."

He wasn't immediately aware of that harsh fact. He had a good life with his grandmother. He felt fully loved and enjoyed many of the same things as other boys in that era.

ON HIS OWN

This happy life ended when he was seven. His grandmother took him to Anthony's farm. Without warning, she abandoned him. He wrote,

❝I fell upon the ground, and wept a boy's bitter tears, refusing to be comforted.❞

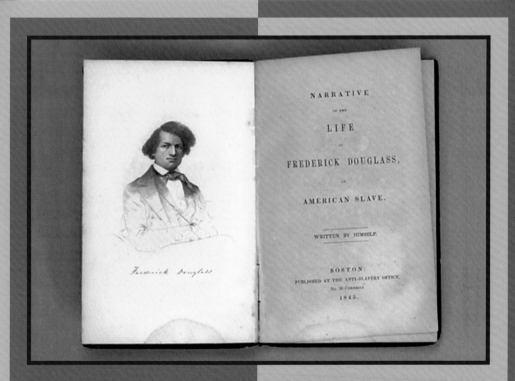

Frederick's book, *Narrative of the Life of Frederick Douglass, an American Slave*, made it clear that his father was a white man. But he never knew his father's name. Frederick wrote, "Slavery had no recognition of fathers." His mother's status as a slave determined his fate as a slave.

A Brief History of Slavery in America

The first African slaves arrived at the Jamestown colony in Virginia in 1619, just 12 years after its founding.

As the population increased, so did the demand for slaves. Most of the demand came from southern states. The southern states had very large plantations with many crops like tobacco, rice, and cotton to be tended to. White plantation owners needed slaves to work for them.

Slaves had almost no rights. They were the property of their masters. Children born to slaves became slaves themselves. Masters bought and sold them. Slave families were often broken up.

By the early 19th century slavery in northern states ended. Tensions about slavery between North and South steadily increased and led to the Civil War.

President Abraham Lincoln issued the Emancipation Proclamation in 1863, freeing the slaves. He worried people might think his action was only temporary. He urged a constitutional amendment to permanently **abolish** it. The Thirteenth Amendment, making slavery illegal in the United States, passed in 1865.

The cook who oversaw the slave children treated Frederick harshly. He had little to eat. Unlike other slave children, he began to question the whole system. He decided someday he would be free.

Frederick soon had a stroke of luck. He was sent to Hugh Auld in Baltimore in 1826. Auld was related to Anthony by marriage. A city slave had a much easier life than field hands. "He is much better fed and clothed, and enjoys privileges altogether unknown to the slave on the plantation," Frederick wrote.

LEARNING TO READ

Auld's wife Sophia liked Frederick. She taught him to read. Auld was furious when he found out. His anger taught Frederick a valuable lesson. Education was the key to freedom. Frederick took every chance to increase his reading and writing ability. He bought a copy of a book filled with famous speeches about human rights. Reading those speeches made him want to be free even more.

His life with the Aulds ended in 1833 when Anthony died. Anthony's slaves were divided up. Frederick now belonged to Thomas Auld, Hugh's brother.

Frederick quickly showed his unhappiness. He refused to refer to Thomas as "Master." Thomas sent him to Edward Covey, a famous "slave breaker." Covey was brutal with slaves who worked for him.

STANDING UP FOR HIMSELF

Frederick endured Covey's beatings for several months. One day he fought back. As he wrote,

> **"This battle with Mr. Covey . . . was the turning point in my *'life as a slave'*. . . . I was nothing before; I WAS A MAN NOW. It recalled to life my crushed self-respect and my self-confidence, and inspired me with a renewed determination to be A FREEMAN."**

Early slave owners branded their slaves, as though they were animals or other property. Slaves were in demand since the earliest American colonies began, but in the 19th century, northern states outlawed slavery. The North and South disagreed about slavery, which was one of the causes of the Civil War.

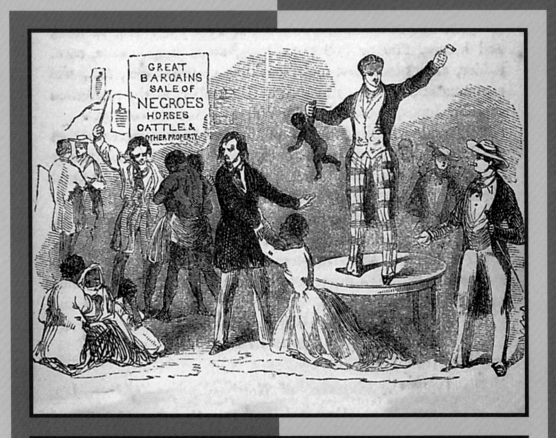

In this illustration, husbands, wives, and families are sold to different purchasers and violently separated, probably never to meet again. Frederick had this experience when his owner died and Frederick was sent to a new master. Harsh treatment led the young slave to plan his escape to the North.

Covey never laid a hand on Frederick again.

Soon afterward, Frederick was sent to a man named William Freeland. Freeland was the complete opposite of Covey. But as Frederick wrote, "I began to want to live *upon free land* as well as *with Freeland*; and I was no longer content, therefore, to live with him or any other slaveholder."

Frederick began making plans to escape.

BECOMING FREE

FREDERICK TALKED FOUR SLAVES INTO joining him in trying to escape. They spent months preparing for the attempt. Unfortunately another slave betrayed them. They were thrown in jail. Frederick feared it was all over:

> **❝I was covered with gloom, sunk down to the utmost despair . . . I thought the possibility of freedom was gone.❞**

Once again Frederick was lucky. Thomas Auld obtained his release and sent him back to his brother Hugh in Baltimore. Auld even said that if Frederick behaved himself, he would free him when he reached the age of 25—seven years away.

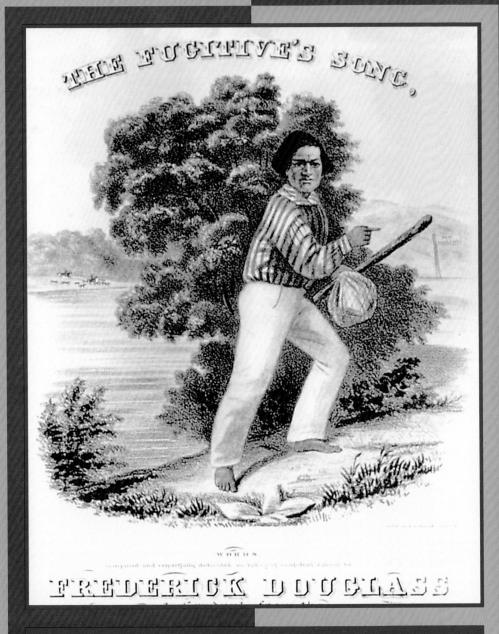

THE FUGITIVE'S SONG,

WORDS

FREDERICK DOUGLASS

"The Fugitive's Song" was a ballad dedicated to Frederick in 1845. Frederick had tired of being treated badly, fled Baltimore, and escaped to New York City. He ended up in Massachusetts and changed his name so it would be harder for slave catchers to find him.

AN UNFAIR ARRANGEMENT

Frederick found work as a **caulker** in a shipyard. He became very skilled and earned good wages. But he had to give his earnings to Hugh Auld. Frederick hated the arrangement and said Auld was no different from a pirate.

Frederick also joined a group of free blacks in Baltimore, where he improved his reading and writing skills. At one of the meetings, he met a black woman named Anna Murray. He soon fell in love with her.

Anna Murray was Frederick's first wife. They met in Baltimore where she was a free black woman. The couple married in New York in 1838, just a few days after Frederick escaped from slavery. Their marriage lasted for 44 years and they had five children.

In many ways he was a free man. But one time he forgot to give his wages to Auld, who was furious. Fearing that Auld might sell him, Frederick decided to escape.

In early September, 1838, Frederick disguised himself as a sailor and boarded a train from Baltimore to Wilmington, Delaware. Though he had plenty of anxious moments, he went from Wilmington to Philadelphia and from there to New York City. As he remembered,

> **"In less than a week after leaving Baltimore, I was walking amid the hurrying throng, and gazing upon the dazzling wonders of Broadway. The dreams of my childhood and the purposes of my manhood were now fulfilled. A free state around me, and a free earth under my feet."**

Anna quickly joined him. They were married on September 15.

Frederick was still in danger. Slave catchers roamed the city's streets. Not even blacks could be trusted. So the couple went to New Bedford, Massachusetts, which was safer. Frederick also wanted to change his last name to make it harder for anyone to track him down.

A NEW NAME

He asked a man who helped him settle in New Bedford to choose his new name. The man had just read *Lady of the Lake*, a long poem by Sir Walter Scott. One of the major characters was named Douglas. Frederick added an extra "s" and created the name by which he would become famous.

Frederick soon realized there was racism in the North, too. He was hired to work as a caulker on a whaling ship. "But upon reaching the float-stage, where the other caulkers were at work, I was told that every white man would leave the ship in her unfinished condition if I struck a blow at my trade upon her," he wrote.

Frederick had to work as a laborer. He did whatever jobs he could find, and made less money than he would have as a caulker.

Still, he got to keep all the money he earned. He needed it. His first child, Rosetta, was born in June, 1839. Lewis came into the world in 1840. Three more children would follow.

By that time, Frederick had begun attending abolitionist meetings and reading the *Liberator*. It was a newspaper published by William Lloyd Garrison, the country's leading abolitionist.

William Lloyd Garrison

William Lloyd Garrison began publishing the weekly abolitionist newspaper, *Liberator*, in 1831. Two years later he helped found the American Anti-Slavery Society.

William believed that the U.S. Constitution was unfair because it allowed slavery. He didn't believe the existing government had the power to abolish slavery. He thought that the northern states should **secede** and form a new nation. Many people disagreed with him. They thought William was too extreme.

Southerners hated him. Many people in the North felt the same way. Sometimes they attacked him when he gave speeches.

In spite of opposition, he kept publishing *Liberator* until the Thirteenth Amendment, which abolished slavery, was passed in 1865. He died in 1879.

What Frederick learned was inspiring:

❝I got a pretty correct idea of the principles, measures and spirit of the anti-slavery reform. I took right hold of the cause. I could do but little; but what I could, I did with a joyful heart, and never felt happier than when in an anti-slavery meeting.❞

Not long afterward Frederick spoke out. Garrison and other abolitionists encouraged him to speak to audiences throughout the northern states. He did that for several years, which led to publication of the *Narrative* and his flight to Great Britain.

FINDING EQUALITY

His reception in Great Britain astonished and pleased him. He was regarded as the equal of anyone whom he met. Perhaps most

William Lloyd Garrison, a famous abolitionist, inspired Frederick through his newspaper, the *Liberator*, which he published for more than 30 years. William encouraged Frederick to speak out against slavery. The two men became friends and attended many anti-slavery meetings together.

remarkable, he could freely walk and talk with white women. Had he done that in the South he would have risked being lynched. For well over a year, he spoke about the evils of slavery to audiences throughout the British Isles.

Despite his fame, Frederick still wanted to come home. "I felt it my duty to labor and suffer with my oppressed people in my native land," he wrote. But if fear of being captured had driven him to cross the Atlantic, now he was a celebrity on two continents. It would be even more dangerous for him to return.

Two English friends solved the problem. They contacted Thomas Auld, who agreed to sell Frederick to his brother. In turn, Hugh Auld agreed to take money in exchange for Frederick's freedom. The friends quickly raised the necessary money and sent it to Auld.

A FREE MAN AT LAST

Frederick Douglass was now a free man. He sailed back to the United States in the spring of 1847.

One of the main reasons he wanted to return to the United States was to start his own newspaper. Several of his English friends contributed more than $2,500.

Not everyone thought this was a good idea. Garrison and other abolitionists disapproved. They thought that another abolitionist newspaper would create unneeded competition for ones already in existence. They pointed out that Frederick didn't have any editorial experience. They questioned if he had enough time to run a newspaper and continue giving speeches. And what if he failed, they said. It wouldn't look good.

Though Frederick was hurt by their objections, he believed in himself strongly enough to move ahead. One reason was the strong belief among many people—in both the North and the South—that blacks were inferior. Of course, Frederick knew otherwise:

> **"A tolerably well-conducted press in the hands of persons of the despised race would, by calling out and making them acquainted with their own latent powers, by enkindling their hope of a future and developing their moral force, prove a most powerful means of removing prejudice and awakening an interest in them."**

Frederick didn't want to compete with the *Liberator*, which was based in Massachusetts. So he moved to Rochester, in western New York. The move reflected a growing split with Garrison. The two men shared the same goal—to end slavery. But they disagreed

Frederick looks elegant in the 1840s, when he returned from England a free man and started his own newspaper in Rochester, New York. He continued to give speeches on slavery reform. Unfortunately his ideas began to clash with those of his old friend, William Lloyd Garrison.

about the best way to do it. Several years later the split would become permanent as Garrison started attacking Frederick in print.

BREAKING INTO PRINT

Frederick began publishing the *North Star* at the end of 1847. He soon found that it was easier to think about publishing a newspaper than to actually do it. Almost immediately the *North Star* had financial problems. Frederick went into debt trying to pay the bills.

Fortunately, Julia Griffiths, whom he had met in England, visited Frederick and offered to help. She was much better at business than Frederick. Soon the paper was out of debt.

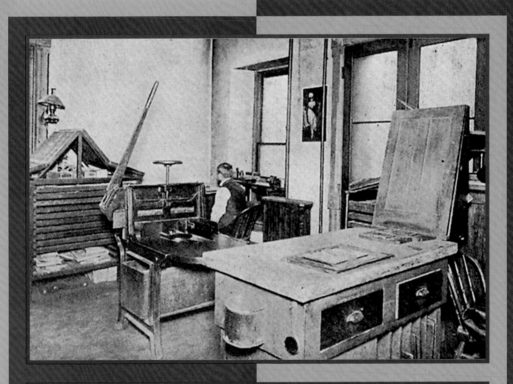

The office of Frederick's newspaper, the *North Star*, was quite basic. But running the newspaper was costly and difficult, and Frederick had to ask a friend to help pay the bills. He used the newspaper to print his ideas about working toward emancipation and promoting women's rights.

Many men in that era wouldn't have accepted help from a woman. Frederick was different. He believed in equal rights for everyone, regardless of sex or race. He attended the first women's rights convention in Seneca Falls, New York, in 1848 and gave a speech in support. Female leaders such as Elizabeth Cady Stanton and Susan B. Anthony were among his lifelong friends.

AN UNFAIR LAW

As if Frederick didn't already have enough to write about in the *North Star*, in 1850 Congress passed the Fugitive Slave Act. Under its terms, people in the North were required to help identify and turn in escaped slaves. To Frederick, it was "a bill undoubtedly more designed to involve the North in **complicity** with slavery and deaden its moral sentiment than to procure the return of fugitives to their so-called owners."

The enactment of the Fugitive Slave Act gave a boost to the Underground Railroad.

The Underground Railroad

The Underground Railroad consisted of thousands of people who helped slaves escape and settle in the North. It didn't have a central organization. Nearly everyone knew only about their location on a journey that took slaves weeks and covered hundreds of miles.

The slaves and their guides, known as "conductors," usually traveled at night between "stations" 10 to 20 miles apart. They hid during the day. While the slaves rested, someone went ahead to the next station to prepare the "stationmaster." Finally they reached a northern state. Many continued to Canada.

Probably the most famous conductor was Harriet Tubman, an escaped slave. Harriet risked her life by making secret trips to the South to aid other slaves in their flight.

No one knows exactly how many slaves escaped using the Underground Railroad. Estimates range from a few thousand to more than 100,000.

Frederick became personally involved. His home became a frequent destination for escaping slaves because it was so close to Canada. Once again he was placing himself in danger:

This painting, *Underground Railroad*, by Charles T. Webber shows a slave family being taken to safety in the snow. Hundreds of people along the "railroad" hid and fed slaves and their guides on their long journey to freedom in the North.

"I could take no step in it without exposing myself to fine and imprisonment. . . . True, as a means of destroying slavery, it was like an attempt to bail out the ocean with a teaspoon, but the thought that there was one *less* slave, and one more freeman . . . brought to my heart unspeakable joy."

In 1851, he merged the *North Star* with another paper, and renamed it *Frederick Douglass' Paper*. The new name reflected his importance in the anti-slavery movement.

"CELEBRATING" THE FOURTH OF JULY

He also continued his heavy speaking schedule. In 1852 Frederick delivered a Fourth of July speech that attracted a great deal of attention. He made sure it reached a wide audience by having it printed. As he said,

> **"What, to the American slave, is your 4th of July? I answer; a day that reveals to him, more than all other days in the year, the gross injustice to which he is the constant victim. To him, your celebration is a sham . . . a thin veil to cover up crimes which would disgrace a nation of savages. . . . For revolting barbarity and shameless hypocrisy, America reigns without a rival."**

In 1855 he published his second autobiography, *My Bondage and My Freedom*. It covered many of the same events as the *Narrative*, but was longer and more detailed.

Two years later, he had even more reason for anger and disgust. The U.S. Supreme Court handed down the *Dred Scott* decision. It declared that slaves were simply the property of their masters. They could never be citizens. Chief Justice Roger Taney wrote that blacks "had no rights which the white man was bound to respect."

While the decision delighted slave owners, it infuriated thousands of people in the North. The divisions between North and South continued to grow.

BREAKING THE COLOR BARRIER

Not all the news was bad. When Frederick and his family originally moved to Rochester, his children weren't allowed to attend white schools. He protested, and his efforts finally paid off when Rochester integrated its schools in 1857.

This depiction of John Brown by Thomas Hovenden shows the famous abolitionist in custody after his failed raid on Harpers Ferry, West Virginia. Although Frederick was a friend of Brown's, he felt a violent raid was wrong. Because some people thought Frederick was involved in the attack, he fled to England.

The nation moved even closer to war in 1859 with John Brown's raid. Frederick had become friends with Brown, a noted abolitionist, more than 10 years earlier. Brown wanted Frederick to be a part of the raid. Frederick thought it was too risky and said no.

John Brown's Raid

John Brown believed in open fighting to end slavery. He planned to attack the federal armory in Harpers Ferry, Virginia. He would give the weapons and ammunition it contained to nearby slaves. They would begin a rebellion in Virginia. From Virginia, the fighting would spread throughout the entire South.

Brown attacked on October 16, 1859. Just one man guarded the armory. He surrendered. Word of the attack quickly got out. Brown had hoped he would have hundreds of men with him. He had only 21. They were quickly pinned down by townspeople and nearby farmers. Soldiers soon arrived and cut off the escape route.

Two days later, with two of his sons dead, Brown surrendered. He was put on trial and hanged a few weeks later.

The raid heightened tensions between the North and South. Many historians believe it became a main cause of the outbreak of the Civil War. Union troops often sang the song "John Brown's Body" while they marched.

When Brown was captured, federal officials thought Frederick had been involved. Even though he hadn't, Frederick doubted he could get a fair trial. He quickly fled to Canada and from there sailed to England.

He returned several months later when his youngest child, Annie, died. By then the 1860 presidential campaign was underway. Frederick knew it would be one of the most important elections in the nation's history.

4

THE CIVIL WAR YEARS

SHORTLY AFTER LINCOLN WON THE presidential election, South Carolina seceded from the Union. Six more states joined South Carolina in February and formed the Confederate States of America.

Frederick had supported Lincoln in his bid for the presidency. He eagerly waited for Lincoln to take office in March to see how he would respond to the crisis:

> "I confess to a feeling allied to satisfaction at the prospect of a conflict between the North and the South. . . . Longing for the end of the bondage of my people, I was ready for any political upheaval which should bring about a change in the existing condition of things."

Frederick seems discouraged in this 1850s portrait. He was disappointed after Abraham Lincoln became president because he hoped Lincoln would be more active in freeing slaves. When the Civil War broke out, Frederick was glad because he thought it would mean a quicker end to slavery.

Abraham Lincoln posed for this portrait around the time he was elected president in 1860. Before the Civil War broke out, Frederick was disappointed that the new president was in favor of keeping slavery in the South and enforcing the Fugitive Slave Act.

A BIG DISAPPOINTMENT

Frederick's hopes took a blow when Lincoln gave his inaugural address. There would be no political upheaval. The president said his main goal was to restore the Union and keep it the way it always had been. He agreed that states that already had slaves could keep them. He promised to enforce the Fugitive Slave Act.

Abraham Lincoln

Abraham Lincoln was born in Kentucky on February 12, 1809, and developed a love of reading at a young age. He became a lawyer in 1836. By then he was involved in politics. He served four terms in the Illinois legislature.

Abraham was elected to the U.S. House of Representatives in 1846. After one term, he returned to his law practice in Springfield, Illinois.

He ran for the U.S. Senate in 1854 and 1858 but lost both times. During the second campaign, he had several debates with Stephen Douglas that made him famous. He used that fame to win the Republican presidential nomination in 1860.

In the election, the Democratic Party split into two factions. Each nominated a candidate. The Constitutional Union Party also had a candidate. Abraham won less than 40 percent of the popular vote but carried 18 states with 180 electoral votes. His rivals combined carried 15 states and 123 electoral votes.

Frederick was disappointed and discouraged. He thought American blacks might be better off if they moved to the Caribbean nation of Haiti. It was a black republic. He planned to travel there for a firsthand look.

Before he could make the trip, Confederate forces opened fire on Fort Sumter, a Union base in South Carolina. Four more states seceded, and the Civil War began.

Frederick was happy with the outbreak of war:

"From the first, I, for one, saw in this war the end of slavery; and truth requires me to say that my interest in the success of the North was largely due to this belief. True it is that this faith was many times shaken by passing events, but never destroyed."

Those passing events sometimes made Frederick wonder whose side Lincoln was on. Union soldiers often returned fleeing slaves to their masters. When Union General John C. Fremont ordered Missouri slaves to be freed, Lincoln overturned the order. Lincoln encouraged blacks to leave the United States and settle elsewhere. And as Frederick wrote, "Mr. Lincoln could tell the poor negro that 'he was the cause of the war.'"

TREADING A FINE LINE

Lincoln was in a difficult position. Four slaveholding states—Delaware, Kentucky, Maryland, and Missouri—still remained in the Union. If these four states joined the Confederacy, it would be a serious blow.

Frederick didn't have much sympathy for Lincoln. He continually made speeches and wrote articles urging Lincoln to free the slaves immediately.

He was disappointed with Lincoln for another reason. The president wouldn't allow blacks to join the Union Army. He feared white Union soldiers wouldn't serve alongside blacks. He also questioned the bravery of blacks. Yet as Frederick pointed out, Southerners were using their blacks to dig trenches, build forts, and other activities that freed Confederate soldiers to fight. "This is no time to fight only with your white hand, and allow your black hand to remain tied," he wrote.

Like many Northerners, Lincoln expected a fairly short war. As it dragged on and thousands of young men on both sides were slaughtered and wounded, Lincoln realized he needed to do something radical to end it.

A FAMOUS DOCUMENT

In the summer of 1862, Lincoln said he would issue the Emancipation Proclamation. It would free all the slaves in the Confederate states. The timing was important. He had to wait for a Union victory on the battlefield. That came in September at the Battle of Antietam. The Emancipation Proclamation was scheduled to take effect on January 1, 1863.

In this painting, Lincoln struggles with writing the Emancipation Proclamation. Frederick and his friends had doubts that Lincoln would enforce the new law. When the proclamation went into effect on January 1, 1863, blacks everywhere joyfully celebrated their new freedom.

Frederick was part of a huge crowd in Boston as the final moments of 1862 ticked away. There was still doubt as to whether Lincoln would do what he had promised. "Hitherto, he had not shown himself a man of heroic measures," Frederick wrote.

Suddenly a man rushed into the crowd, shouting, "It [the Emancipation Proclamation] is coming! It is on the wires!!"

Frederick wrote,

"The effect of this announcement was startling beyond description, and the scene was wild and grand. Joy and gladness exhausted all forms or expression, from shouts of praise to sobs and tears."

As part of the Emancipation Proclamation, Lincoln said blacks could serve in the Union army. Frederick immediately devoted his vast energy to recruiting men for the cause. As he wrote to young black men in *Frederick Douglass' Paper* and had widely reprinted,

"This is your hour and mine. . . . I urge you to fly to arms, and smite with death the power that would bury the government and your liberty in the same hopeless grave. . . . This is our golden opportunity. Let us accept it and forever wipe out the dark reproaches unsparingly hurled against us by our enemies."

JOINING THE ARMY

Frederick's son Lewis joined the 54th Massachusetts Volunteer Infantry. The unit showed how brave black soldiers could be at the Battle of Fort Wagner. Lewis was fortunate to survive.

The Attack on Fort Wagner

In July, 1863, Union troops tried to capture Fort Wagner. It was a Confederate fort on an island near Charleston, South Carolina.

The 54th Massachusetts Volunteers led the attack. The regiment was the first black unit in the Union army. Its officers were whites, led by Colonel Robert Gould Shaw.

Shaw led his 600 men forward along a narrow beach. Confederate guns firing at point-blank range killed Shaw and 116 men. Another 156 were wounded. Along with other Union troops, they captured part of the fort. But they couldn't hold on. They retreated.

Though the attack failed, it proved black troops were just as courageous as whites. Union officials recruited many more blacks. Eventually blacks made up nearly 10 percent of Union military and naval forces.

The battle inspired the 1989 movie *Glory*. The film won three Academy Awards, including Denzel Washington's Oscar for best supporting actor.

It didn't take long for problems to emerge. Black soldiers were paid much less than whites. Their equipment wasn't as good. They couldn't become officers. And the Confederates made it very clear that blacks would be shot or hanged if they surrendered.

Frederick stopped recruiting. He met with Lincoln in August 1863, to try to solve those problems. While the meeting wasn't as satisfactory as Frederick had hoped, it did convince him to resume his recruiting efforts.

MEETING LINCOLN AGAIN

Frederick also began thinking about what would happen after the war. It wasn't enough to free the slaves. He wanted them to be full citizens. He was especially concerned about voting rights. He wasn't sure that Lincoln was the right man to achieve those goals.

In May 1864, he was among many people who supported John C. Fremont as president. Among other things, Fremont guaranteed

Soldiers of the 107th United States Colored Infantry pose for a photo. During the Civil War, more than 200,000 blacks enlisted in the Union army, accounting for 10 percent of the North's troops. Frederick was tireless in his efforts to prove that blacks could be as good soldiers as whites.

that he would pursue the war until victory was achieved and propose a constitutional amendment outlawing slavery. The Republicans, now the National Unity Party, renominated Lincoln.

To Frederick's horror, the Democrats nominated George McClellan, one of Lincoln's former generals. McClellan favored an immediate peace. That meant slaves would not be free. Frederick and most of Fremont's supporters quickly switched their support to Lincoln. Fremont withdrew from the race.

President Lincoln gives his second inaugural speech, 1865. Lincoln invited Frederick to his inaugural celebration at the White House, but Frederick was turned away at first because he was black. He got word to Lincoln, who then welcomed him in front of all the other guests.

Soon afterward, Lincoln invited Frederick for a second meeting. The president was exhausted. He asked Frederick to draw up a plan that would lead as many slaves as possible to Union lines if he decided he couldn't win the war. Frederick came away with a greater understanding of the huge burdens Lincoln faced.

WINNING THE WAR—AT LAST

Events made the plan unnecessary. Lincoln easily won re-election in November. Soon afterward, Union General William T. Sherman began the famous "March to the Sea" that cut the Confederacy in half.

Lincoln invited Frederick to the inaugural celebration at the White House in March, 1865. When he tried to enter, guards turned him away. Frederick got word of the snub to Lincoln, who ordered the guards to admit him. Frederick wrote:

> " Recognizing me, even before I reached him, [Lincoln] exclaimed, so that all around could hear him, 'Here comes my friend Douglass.' "

It was among the president's last acts of generosity. Lincoln was assassinated on April 14, five days after the Confederate surrender. By then, Frederick's previous doubts and disagreements had disappeared:

> " Mr. Lincoln was not only a great President, but a GREAT MAN—too great to be small in anything. In his company I never in any way reminded of my humble origin, or my unpopular color. "

Frederick hoped that Lincoln's legacy would live on. There was one positive sign. The Thirteenth Amendment, which abolished slavery everywhere in the United States, was ratified in December, 1865.

But as Frederick would soon discover, a long and bitter struggle was about to begin.

Chapter
5

❀

A LONG AND FULFILLING LIFE

FREDERICK HAD DEVOTED HIS ENERGIES for many years to ending slavery. With that goal accomplished, Frederick wasn't sure what to do next. His first thought was to "purchase a little farm and settle myself down to earn an honest living by tilling the soil."

Frederick would never become a farmer. He soon realized that his work had just begun.

The South had lost the Civil War. But Southerners continued to fight against rights for blacks. It seemed that Andrew Johnson, Lincoln's successor as president, was helping them. Frederick had had a revealing glimpse of Johnson at Lincoln's second inauguration. Lincoln turned to Johnson and pointed out Frederick to him:

Frederick posed for many photos during his long and productive life. After the Civil War, he thought he would retire and live quietly. Then he realized he needed to continue his work to ensure passage of the constitutional amendments that gave more rights to blacks.

> "The first expression which came to his [Johnson's] face, and which I think was the true index of his heart, was one of bitter contempt and aversion. Seeing that I observed him, he tried to assume a more friendly appearance, but it was too late. . . . I turned to Mrs. Dorsey [a friend] and said, 'Whatever Andrew Johnson may be, he certainly is no friend of our race.'"

GUARANTEEING RIGHTS

Johnson quickly proved that Frederick was right. Many members of Congress agreed with Frederick. They took on increasing power at Johnson's expense. In 1866 Congress passed the Fourteenth Amendment, which guaranteed certain rights to blacks. It was **ratified** two years later.

Frederick supported Republican Ulysses S. Grant for president in 1868. Black votes played a vital role in Grant's election.

Ulysses S. Grant

Ulysses S. Grant was born in 1822. He fought in the Mexican-American War (1846-1848) and left the army in 1854. He had several different jobs but didn't do well at any of them.

The Civil War changed Grant's life. He was named colonel of an Illinois regiment and soon promoted to brigadier general. Lincoln appointed him general-in-chief of the Union army in 1864. He received the Confederate surrender the following year.

Many historians don't rate him very highly as president. Grant personally was honest but he put too much trust in men who were not. In recent years his reputation has improved because he supported rights for blacks.

After leaving the White House, Grant went bankrupt. He also contracted cancer. To leave his family with enough money, he quickly wrote an autobiography. He finished it just before his death in 1885 and it was very successful.

Grant pushed the Fifteenth Amendment, which stated, "The right of citizens of the United States to vote shall not be denied or **abridged** by the United States or by any State on account of race, color, or previous condition of servitude."

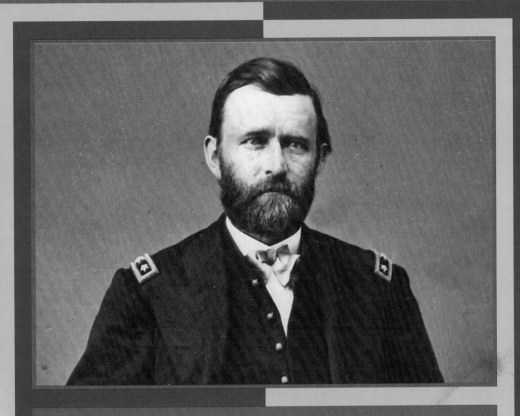

Former Civil War general Ulysses S. Grant was elected president in 1868, thanks in part to Frederick's support. Grant later championed the Fifteenth Amendment, which gave blacks the right to vote. He also appointed Frederick to a commission to look into annexing Santo Domingo as part of the U.S.

The Fifteenth Amendment was adopted in 1870. Its effects quickly became apparent. Many blacks were elected to state offices and a few to Congress.

ANOTHER NEWSPAPER

In 1870 Frederick became editor of the *New Era* newspaper. The paper soon experienced financial problems. Frederick bought out the owners and renamed it the *New National Era*. This time there was no Julia Griffiths to help out. After costing Frederick thousands of dollars, the paper folded in 1874.

In 1871, Grant appointed Frederick as a member of a commission that sailed to Santo Domingo (modern-day Dominican Republic) to look into the possibility of annexing the country as part of the United States. Frederick loved the idea of "a black sister of Massachusetts." While nothing came of the proposal, to Frederick being on the commission was a symbol of the changes that freedom brought:

> **"It placed me on the deck of an American man-of-war, manned by one hundred marines and five hundred men-of-wars men, under the national flag, which I could now call mine, in common with other American citizens, and gave me a place not in the fore-castle, among the hands, nor in the caboose with the cooks, but in the captain's saloon and in the society of gentlemen, scientists, and statesmen."**

His house in Rochester burned down the following year. He decided not to rebuild. Instead he moved his family to Washington, D.C. to be closer to political activity.

VICE PRESIDENT? SORRY, NOT INTERESTED

The Equal Rights Party nominated Victoria Woodhull for president in 1872 and Frederick for vice president. No one asked Frederick if he wanted the position. He didn't, because he supported Grant's re-election. Grant easily won. Frederick was named as one of two electors-at-large from New York. He and another man took the state's election results to the capitol.

Two years later he was named president of the Freedmen's Savings and Trust Company, which held the savings of many blacks. The previous administrators had badly weakened it. Frederick spent thousands of dollars of his own money but the bank still failed. Thousands of blacks lost their money.

Frederick needed to earn money to make up for his financial losses. He began giving lectures again. With interest in slavery decreasing, he spoke on many other topics.

This poster, titled "Heroes of the Colored Race," features Frederick between the only two African Americans to serve as U.S. senators in the 19th century. He remained an important voice for the future of equal rights and was delighted to see blacks and whites together in the crowd when he spoke.

MAKING PROGRESS

One of his most famous speeches was the dedication of the Freedmen's Monument in Washington, D.C., in 1876. To Frederick, seeing whites and blacks mingling freely was a sign of progress:

> **Few facts could better illustrate the vast and wonderful change which has taken place in our condition as a people than the fact of our assembling here for the purpose we have today. Harmless, beautiful, proper, and praiseworthy as this demonstration is,**

I cannot forget that no such demonstration would have been tolerated here twenty years ago. . . . [It is] a prophecy of still greater national enlightenment and progress in the future."

Events soon showed that Frederick's optimism about the future was misplaced.

The election of Rutherford B. Hayes in 1876 benefited Frederick personally. Hayes appointed Frederick as marshal of Washington, D.C. the following year. Soon afterward, Frederick traveled to Maryland to the places he had been a slave. He visited Thomas Auld, his old master. The men parted on good terms. Frederick also purchased an estate in Washington, D.C. called Cedar Hill.

Black citizens pay their respects to Frederick in his marshal's office in Washington, D.C., 1877. Frederick was appointed to well-paid jobs by presidents Hayes and Garfield. For the first time he had enough time and money to make speeches and work on his third autobiography.

But Hayes ended Reconstruction. Most blacks didn't have any property. Many were forced to work for their former masters as sharecroppers. Their condition wasn't much better than it had been when they were slaves.

Reconstruction

When the Civil War ended, the South had to rebuild its economy and government. President Johnson wanted to quickly restore governments in southern states, without much protection for blacks. Congress disagreed. It passed the Reconstruction Act. The Act created five military districts, in which soldiers would protect blacks. It also required southern states to allow all men to vote regardless of race.

Many Southerners were unhappy. The Ku Klux Klan and other groups murdered blacks and white supporters. Reconstruction also became increasingly unpopular in the North.

Democrat Samuel Tilden won the popular vote in the 1876 presidential election. But the vote was in doubt in three southern states. A Congressional committee worked out a deal. They gave the three states to Hayes, which ensured his election. In return, Hayes ended Reconstruction when he took office in 1877 and withdrew federal troops.

The end of Reconstruction allowed the southern states to form white supremacist governments. These governments quickly stripped blacks of most of the rights they had just gained.

Soon after James Garfield was elected president in 1880, he appointed Frederick as recorder of deeds in Washington, D.C. The job paid Frederick a good income. It also gave him time for writing and speaking. He published his third autobiography, *Life and Times of Frederick Douglass*, in 1881. It was the longest and most complete.

A New Marriage

Frederick suffered a severe personal blow the following year. His wife Anna died after a long illness. Throughout their marriage, Anna managed the household and took care of the children. She dealt with his long absences from home.

A year and a half later, Frederick married Helen Pitts, his personal secretary. Helen was nearly 20 years younger than Frederick. She was also white.

Frederick sits with his second wife Helen (right) and her sister Eva. When some people criticized him for marrying a white woman, Frederick joked that his first wife was the color of his mother and the second was the color of his father.

The marriage generated a great amount of criticism. Many people disapproved of interracial marriages. Even the families were opposed. Helen's father refused to speak to her. Frederick's adult children were only a few years younger than Helen. They found it hard to accept her.

Frederick and Helen genuinely loved each other and were very happy. Frederick was angry at people who criticized his marriage:

"People who had remained silent over the unlawful relations of the white slave masters with their colored slave women loudly condemned me for marrying a wife a few shades lighter than myself."

He also took a more humorous approach:

"This proves I am impartial. My first wife was the color of my mother and the second, the color of my father."

He and Helen took an extended European trip in 1886. Two years later he toured the South. He realized that his comfortable lifestyle had blinded him to living conditions for most blacks. He began speaking out on their behalf. One time he criticized "so-called **emancipation** as a stupendous fraud."

In 1889 President Benjamin Harrison appointed Frederick as consul-general to Haiti. Frederick served there for two years.

Haiti

Haiti occupies the western third of the Caribbean island of Hispaniola, which Columbus discovered in 1492. Spanish settlers soon swarmed to the island. Overwork and disease killed nearly all the original Taino Indians. African slaves replaced them.

France and Spain divided Hispaniola in 1697. The French controlled what they named Saint-Domingue. Thriving sugar and coffee plantations made Saint-Domingue very wealthy.

French planters treated their slaves brutally. A revolt began in 1791 and achieved independence in 1804. The victorious slaves, now free, renamed their country Haiti. It was the only country to become independent due to a slave revolt.

Haiti has rarely known political stability. Internal conflicts are one reason. Interference by foreign countries such as France and the United States is another. A series of dictators is a third.

Today, Haiti is one of the world's poorest countries. Nearly half its people can't read or write. Most of the original forests have been cut down. That creates soil erosion and flooding.

When Frederick returned, he turned his attention to the epidemic of lynching that was sweeping the South. More than 100 blacks were lynched in 1891 alone. Frederick continually

Frederick's death was memorialized in this funeral music. Today he is remembered for his powerful speeches, which have been compared with those of Martin Luther King, Jr. Long before the civil rights movement of the 1960s, Frederick worked tirelessly toward justice and equality for all people, regardless of their gender or race.

spoke out against the barbaric practice. He also begged Harrison to introduce anti-lynching legislation. The president refused.

A HIGH HONOR

In 1893 Haiti appointed Frederick as its representative at the Columbian Exposition in Chicago. The exposition honored the 400th anniversary of Columbus' discovery of the New World. Frederick regarded this appointment as one of the highest honors of his life. He was the only black American to serve in an official role at the Exposition.

On February 20, 1895, Frederick went to a meeting of women's rights activists in Washington, D.C. That evening, he was discussing the event with Helen. Suddenly he suffered a massive heart attack and died.

Today he is regarded as one of the towering figures in black history. He dedicated virtually his entire life to advancing the cause of freedom and equality, not just for blacks but for everyone. No other black man of his era had a more powerful effect.

A GREAT SPEAKER

Of all his gifts, perhaps the most powerful was his speaking ability. Without doubt, he was at least the equal of Dr. Martin Luther King Jr. in his ability to move audiences. One of his longtime friends, women's rights crusader Elizabeth Cady Stanton, said,

> "He stood there like an African prince, majestic in his wrath. Around him sat the great antislavery orators of the day, earnestly watching the effect of his **eloquence** on that immense audience, that laughed and wept by turns, completely carried away by the wondrous gifts of his pathos and humor. On this occasion, all the other speakers seemed tame after Frederick Douglass."

Frederick Douglass is one of the true giants of the civil rights movement. He continues to serve as an inspiration for countless numbers of people, regardless of their race.

1817 or 1818	Born as a slave in February on plantation in Maryland; lives with grandmother.
1824	Separated from grandmother and sent to farm of Aaron Anthony.
1826	Sent to Baltimore to work for Hugh Auld.
1833	Sent back to Anthony to work for Thomas Auld.
1834	Works for Edward Covey.
1835	Works for William Freeland.
1836	Tries to escape but is betrayed and put in jail; returns to Hugh Auld when released and works in Baltimore shipyard as caulker.
1838	Escapes to New York; marries Anna Murray; changes name to Douglass.
1839	Daughter Rosetta is Born.
1840	Son Lewis is Born.
1841	Speaks at meeting of American Anti-Slavery Society; is asked to go on lecture tour.
1842	Son Frederick Jr. is Born.
1844	Son Charles is Born.
1845	Publishes first autobiography, *Narrative of the Life of Frederick Douglass*; flees to England thereafter for fear of being captured and returned to Maryland to his owner.
1846	English supporters raise money to buy his freedom; becomes a free man.
1847	Returns to United States; moves to Rochester, New York; starts publishing *North Star*.
1848	Attends women's rights convention.
1849	Daughter Annie is born.
1850	Begins involvement with the Underground Railroad.
1851	Changes name of *North Star* to *Frederick Douglass' Paper*.

1852   Delivers Fourth of July speech criticizing U.S. acceptance of slavery.

1855   Publishes second autobiography, *My Bondage and My Freedom*.

1859   Flees to Canada and then to England after failure of John Brown's raid.

1860   Returns to United States after learning of death of daughter Annie the previous year.

1861   Calls for use of black troops in Union Army.

1863   Meets with Abraham Lincoln to discuss treatment of black soldiers.

1864   Meets with Lincoln the second time.

1866   Meets with President Andrew Johnson to protest the new president's policies.

1872   Moves family to Washington D.C. when his home in Rochester burns down.

1876   Speaks at dedication of Freedmen's Monument.

1877   Returns to Maryland and visits Thomas Auld, his former owner.

1878   Purchases Cedar Hill, a nine-acre estate in Washington, D.C.

1881   Publishes third autobiography, *Life and Times of Frederick Douglass*.

1882   Wife Anna dies.

1884   Marries Helen Pitts.

1886   Takes extended tour of Europe.

1891   Returns to United States after two years in Haiti.

1892   Issues revised edition of *Life and Times of Frederick Douglass*.

1895   Dies on February 20 in Washington, D.C.

1845   Publishes first autobiography, *Narrative of the Life of Frederick Douglass*.

1852   Serves as vice president of Liberty Party convention.

1855   Publishes second autobiography, *My Bondage and My Freedom*.

1857   Desegregates schools in Rochester.

1870   Becomes first black reporter allowed into U.S. Capitol press galleries.

Becomes editor of the *New Era*.

1871   Appointed to commission to study the possibility of annexing Santo Domingo to the United States.

1872   Nominated for vice-president by Equal Rights Party on a ticket headed by Victoria Woodhull.

Named as one of two electors-at-large from New York, carrying results of state's presidential voting to Washington, D.C.

1874   Becomes president of Freedman's Savings and Trust Company but it quickly fails.

1877   Appointed marshal of Washington, D.C.

1880   Appointed as recorder of deeds in Washington, D.C.

1881   Publishes third autobiography, *Life and Times of Frederick Douglass*.

1889   Named consul-general to Haiti.

1892   Issues revised edition of *Life and Times of Frederick Douglass*.

1893   Haiti appoints him as the country's representative to Columbian Exposition in Chicago.

1899   Rochester erects statue of Frederick Douglass.

1943   Liberty ship SS Frederick Douglass is launched.

1967   U.S. Postal Service issues a 25-cent first class stamp with a picture of Frederick Douglass.

1986   University of Rochester establishes Frederick Douglass Institute for African and African-American Studies.

1995   U.S. Postal Service issues a block of 20 first-class stamps based on theme of "Civil War, 1861-1865, The War Between the States" that includes Frederick Douglass.

2007   Committee of reporters that controls access to Capitol press galleries dedicates a plaque and portrait of Frederick Douglass.

2009   Frederick Douglass memorial marker dedicated in Jackson Park, Chicago.

abolish—do away with, eliminate.

abridged—reduced, shortened.

brethren—fellow members of a group.

caulker—person who fills in the gaps between planks on wooden ships to make them watertight.

complicity—being part of a shameful or wrongful action.

eloquence—speaking or writing that is especially forceful and moving.

emancipation—the action of freeing from slavery or bondage.

fore-castle—area in the front of a ship where crew members have their living quarters; usually very cramped.

latent—something present but which hasn't been developed yet.

orator—a very good public speaker.

ratified—approved.

refute—prove that something is wrong or false.

secede—withdraw, stop being a part of something.

sham—something false.

skeptical—doubting that something is true.

sunder—split into two parts.

Books and Periodicals

Haugen, Brenda. *Frederick Douglass: Slave, Writer, Abolitionist* (Signature Lives). Mankato, Minnesota: Compass Point Books, 2005.

Ruffin, Frances E. *Sterling Biographies: Frederick Douglass: Rising Up from Slavery*. New York: Sterling Publishing, 2008.

Russell, Sharman Apt. *Frederick Douglass: Abolitionist Editor* (Black Americans of Achievement). Philadelphia: Chelsea House, 2005.

Schuman, Michael A. *Frederick Douglass: Truth Is of No Color* (Americans the Spirit of a Nation). Berkeley Heights, New Jersey: Enslow, 2009.

Sterngrass, Jon. *Frederick Douglas* (Leaders of the Civil War Era). Philadelphia: Chelsea House, 2009.

Web Sites

http://www.nps.gov/archive/frdo/freddoug.html

The Frederick Douglass National Historic Site offers a guide and virtual tour of Cedar Hill, Frederick Douglass's final home; it also includes his biography.

http://www.hstc.org/frederickdouglass.htm

This Web site has a biography of Frederick Douglass, with particular emphasis on his birth and early years in Talbot County, Maryland.

http://www.americaslibrary.gov/cgi-bin/page.cgi/aa/activists/douglass

Several brief stories about Frederick Douglass appear on this site, including details of his 1838 escape.

http://www.youtube.com/watch?v=mb_sqh577Zw

In this clip, actor Danny Glover reads Frederick Douglass's 1852 Fourth of July speech.

http://www.enotes.com/authors/frederick-douglass

This Web site includes Frederick Douglass photos, resources, and numerous links.

page

2: LOC/NMI	30: LOC/NMI
6: LOC/PRMM	32: LOC/NMI
9: LOC/PRMM	35: LOC/NMI
11: LOC/NMI	36: LOC/NMI
12: New Millennium Images	39: LOC/NMI
15: New Millennium Images	41: LOC/NMI
16: LOC/NMI	42: LOC/NMI
18: New Millennium Images	45: LOC/NMI
19: New Millennium Images	47: LOC/NMI
21: New Millennium Images	49: LOC/NMI
22: LOC/NMI	50: LOC/NMI
25: LOC/NMI	52: LOC/NMI
27: LOC/PRMM	54: LOC/NMI
28: LOC/PRMM	

Front cover: LOC/NMI

ABOUT THE AUTHOR

Jim Whiting has written more than 100 children's non-fiction books and edited well over 150 more during an especially diverse writing career. He published *Northwest Runner* magazine for more than 17 years. His other credits include advising a national award-winning high school newspaper, sports editor for the *Bainbridge Island Review*, event and venue write-ups and photography for American Online, articles in dozens of magazines, light verse in the *Saturday Evening Post*, the first piece of original fiction to appear in *Runner's World*, and official photographer for the Antarctica Marathon. His other Mason Crest titles include *American Idol Judges*, *Troy Polamalu*, *David Beckham*, *Hilary Duff*, and *Mandy Moore*.